MINERVA LOUISE

on Christmas Eve

MINERVA LOUISE

on Christmas Eve

Janet Morgan Stoeke

PUFFIN BOOKS

For Brenda

PUFFIN BOOKS
Published by the Penguin Group
Penguin Young Readers Group, 345 Hudson Street, New York, New York 10014, U.S.A.
Penguin Group (Canada), 90 Eglinton Avenue East, Suite 700, Toronto, Ontario, Canada M4P 2Y3 (a division of Pearson Penguin Canada Inc.)
Penguin Books Ltd, 80 Strand, London WC2R 0RL, England
Penguin Ireland, 25 St Stephen's Green, Dublin 2, Ireland (a division of Penguin Books Ltd)
Penguin Group (Australia), 250 Camberwell Road, Camberwell, Victoria 3124, Australia (a division of Pearson Australia Group Pty Ltd)
Penguin Books India Pvt Ltd, 11 Community Centre, Panchsheel Park, New Delhi - 110 017, India
Penguin Group (NZ), 67 Apollo Drive, Rosedale, North Shore 0632, New Zealand (a division of Pearson New Zealand Ltd)
Penguin Books (South Africa) (Pty) Ltd, 24 Sturdee Avenue, Rosebank, Johannesburg 2196, South Africa

Registered Offices: Penguin Books Ltd, 80 Strand, London WC2R 0RL, England

First published in the United States of America by Dutton Children's Books, a division of Penguin Young Readers Group, 2007
Published by Puffin Books, a division of Penguin Young Readers Group, 2009

1 3 5 7 9 10 8 6 4 2

Text and illustrations copyright © Janet Morgan Stoeke, 2007
All rights reserved

THE LIBRARY OF CONGRESS HAS CATALOGED THE DUTTON CHILDREN'S BOOKS EDITION AS FOLLOWS:
Stoeke, Janet Morgan.
Minerva Louise on Christmas Eve / Janet Morgan Stoeke.— 1st ed.
p. cm.
Summary: Minerva Louise follows a farmer in a red hat from a snowy rooftop, down a "well," and into the house with the red curtains, where she finds a tree decorated with sparkling eggs.
ISBN: 978-0-525-47857-7 (hc)
[1. Chickens—Fiction. 2. Christmas—Fiction. 3. Santa Claus—Fiction.] I. Title.
PZ7.S8696Mlm 2007 [E]—dc22 2006035907

Puffin Books ISBN 978-0-14-241449-1

Designed by Abby Kuperstock

Manufactured in China

Minerva Louise loved the way the snow
sparkled on the house with the red curtains.

Hey, those aren't just sparkles, she said.
They're fireflies!

And they're all dressed up in party colors!
What fun!

The party must be up here on the roof.
Oh look, they've invited some goats.

And the goats have put on their *fanciest* horns
for the party. Hey, who else is here?

Oh, it's a farmer in a red hat.

Hello, Mr. Farmer!
How did you get up here?

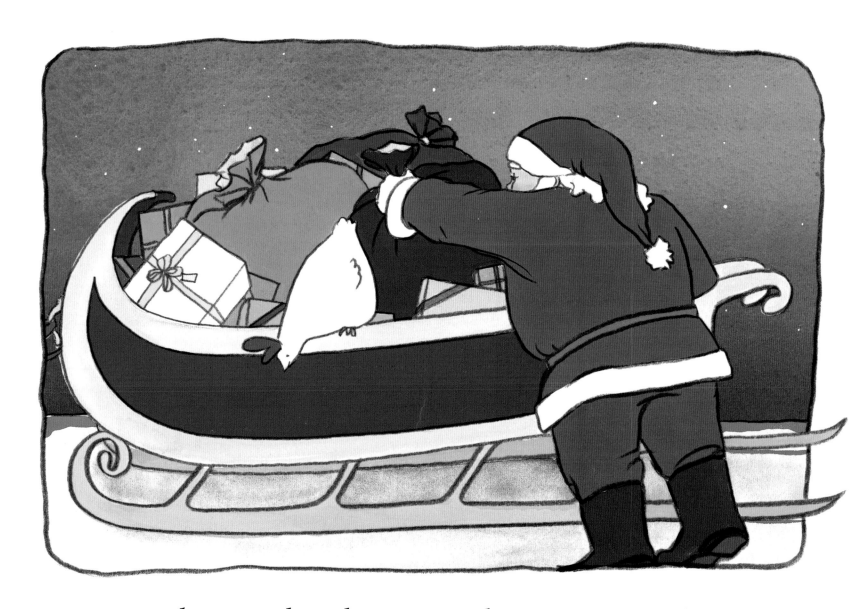

Whoa! What happened to your truck?
Did all the wheels fall off?

You know, it is kind of slippery up here.
Be careful you don't fall.

Oh, dear. I knew you'd fall. Minerva Louise
jumped down into the well after him.

She landed with a dusty PLOP! into
a nest she had seen before.

Oh! I must be inside, she thought.

Wait a minute. That tree wasn't in here before.
It must have come in out of the cold.

Oh, and that pretty white hen is
sitting up there to warm it up.

Look! She's been laying the most *beautiful* eggs!
They are all over the branches.

Hey, Mr. Farmer, what are you doing? Unpacking?

But this is where *my* farmers live.
Now take your stuff out of their socks!

And don't eat that! It's their breakfast!
What will my farmers say when they wake up?

You tell him, she whispered.
He's not listening to me.

The farmer in the red hat just looked at her and smiled. Then he pulled something from his bag.

For *me*? Minerva Louise was so thrilled.

She just *loved* presents!